Acting Edition

Dig

by Theresa Rebeck

FOR PRODUCTION INQUIRIES

UNITED STATES AND CANADA
info@concordtheatricals.com
1-866-979-0447

UNITED KINGDOM AND EUROPE
licensing@concordtheatricals.co.uk
020-7054-7298

Each title is subject to availability from Concord Theatricals Corp., depending upon country of performance. Please be aware that *DIG* may not be licensed by Concord Theatricals Corp. in your territory. Professional and amateur producers should contact the nearest Concord Theatricals Corp. office or licensing partner to verify availability.

No one shall make any changes in this title(s) for the purpose of production. No part of this book may be reproduced, stored in a retrieval system, scanned, uploaded, or transmitted in any form, by any means, now known or yet to be invented, including mechanical, electronic, digital, photocopying, recording, videotaping, or otherwise, without the prior written permission of the publisher. No one shall share this title(s), or any part of this title(s), through any social media or file hosting websites.

For all inquiries regarding motion picture, television, online/digital and other media rights, please contact Concord Theatricals Corp.

MUSIC AND THIRD-PARTY MATERIALS USE NOTE

Licensees are solely responsible for obtaining formal written permission from copyright owners to use copyrighted music and/or other copyrighted third-party materials (e.g. artworks, logos) in the performance of this play and are strongly cautioned to do so. If no such permission is obtained by the licensee, then the licensee must use only original music and materials that the licensee owns and controls. Licensees are solely responsible and liable for clearances of all third-party copyrighted materials, including without limitation music, and shall indemnify the copyright owners of the play(s) and their licensing agent, Concord Theatricals Corp., against any costs, expenses, losses and liabilities arising from the use of such copyrighted third-party materials by licensees. For music, please contact the appropriate music licensing authority in your territory for the rights to any incidental music.

IMPORTANT BILLING AND CREDIT REQUIREMENTS

If you have obtained performance rights to this title, please refer to your licensing agreement for important billing and credit requirements.

DIG was originally produced by the Dorset Theatre Festival (Dina Janis, Artistic Director) in Dorset, Vermont, in July 2019. The performance was directed by Theresa Rebeck, with sets by Christopher and Justin Swader, lights by Mary Ellen Stebbins, costumes by Fabian Aguilar, and sound by Fitz Patton. The production stage manager was Avery Trunko. The cast was as follows:

ROGER	Jeffrey Bean
LOU	Triney Sandoval
MEGAN	Andrea Syglowski
MOLLY	Sarah Stephens
EVERETT	Greg Keller
ADAM	David Mason

DIG received its New York premiere at Primary Stages (Shane D. Hudson, Executive Director; Erin Daley, Interim Artistic Director; Casey Childs, Founder) at 59e59 Theatres in New York City, in September 2023, with the same cast.

DIG was originally commissioned by South Coast Repertory (David Ivers, Artistic Director; Paula Tomei, Managing Director).

CHARACTERS

ROGER – 54, the owner of the shop, a bit of a crank.

LOU – 60, Hispanic. He is broken, wounded, defensive. Roger's best friend and Megan's father.

MEGAN – 34, a ferocious wound, striving to survive.

MOLLY – 20s–30s, a lovely, talkative outsider.

EVERETT – late 20s–mid-30s, a persistent slacker.

ADAM – 35, impatient alpha male.

Casting Note

All parts aside from Lou can be cast as any race.

SETTING

A dying street in a decent-sized city.
Atlanta, or Albany, or Pittsburgh, someplace like that.

TIME

Present, or thereabouts.

ACT ONE

(A cluttered shop. There are a lot of plants but a little too much space. Quite green quite lonely. A skylight and a cash register. In the back, a door to another space.)

(The front door, which exits to the street, has the name of the store on it: Dig. Because we are looking at it from inside, it is backwards.)

*(On the table, center, is a large nearly-dead elephant ear. It is in terrible shape. **ROGER**, fifty-four, the owner of the shop, considers it. He is shrewd, focused, but reactive, annoyed. He is a little like a cactus. Beside him, **LOU**, sixty, less like a cactus and more like someone who's just flat-out reactive. **ROGER** turns the plant. **MEGAN**, thirty-four, pissed, leans against the front window, looking out the door. She has visible tattoos.)*

ROGER. It's not good.

LOU. I'm aware.

ROGER. The soil is...

LOU. I watered it.

ROGER. You didn't.

LOU. Okay, there was a period where watering was not my central focus.

ROGER. "Focus."

LOU. Focus is the wrong word.

ROGER. Focus is no word, it doesn't apply at all, there is no indication that focus had anything to do with the care of this plant.

LOU. I didn't water it for a little while, I know that was damaging.

ROGER. Damaging?

> (*He shakes his head at the shockingly self-serving inaccuracy of this word.* **MEGAN** *watches these guys go at each other.*)

LOU. I brought it to you for help. I understand this is not ideal. I did not neglect this plant.

ROGER. This plant that I gave you

LOU. Come on, I feel bad. I feel really bad. I did water it, mostly, and then I forgot and it was not looking great

ROGER. No when you don't water a plant they tend to feel it.

LOU. – but then I DID water it, I tried to help it. I was aware

ROGER. You doused it.

LOU. It needed water, so I fed it.

ROGER. With the plant food I gave you?

LOU. I did, yes.

> (*Pause.* **ROGER** *looks at him.*)

Okay. I don't understand the concept of plant food.

ROGER. It's food for the plant.

LOU. Okay. I know that makes sense to you.

ROGER. So when so when

LOU. Okay

ROGER. So when you say "I fed this plant" what you mean

LOU. I watered it.

ROGER. You didn't water it!

LOU. I did water it.

ROGER. After you didn't. You didn't water it for let's say a month

LOU. It wasn't that

ROGER. Are you going to tell me

LOU. It was a while.

ROGER. So you didn't water the plant for a month, and then it was clearly, it made its presence known to you with the fact that it was – not dying, but failing. Failing miserably.

LOU. Okay

ROGER. At which point you poured water on it and drowned it. To help it along.

> *(There is a terrible moment. **LOU** cannot answer this. **ROGER** turns away, utterly frustrated.)*

LOU. I apologize.

ROGER. *(Renewed frustration.)* You APOLOGIZE?

LOU. What do you want?

ROGER. I don't want, I don't – never mind. It's fine. I will save this plant.

LOU. You can save it?

ROGER. Just don't talk to me for a minute, okay?

> *(He takes the plant to a plant stand. He places it there and turns it. **LOU** watches him, embarrassed. **ROGER** ignores him.)*

LOU. Where is that kid with the coffee?

ROGER. The lines over there are long sometimes.

LOU. I don't know why you hired that kid.

ROGER. I needed someone to help with the truck.

LOU. You're letting him drive that truck, that seems insane to me.

ROGER. You don't get a vote.

LOU. I'm your accountant.

ROGER. You're not my accountant. Not by any stretch of the imagination are you my accountant.

LOU. I help with the books.

ROGER. Occasionally, you help with the books.

LOU. More than occasionally. And I'm telling you, you can't afford that kid.

ROGER. Someone has to drive the truck.

LOU. He drives that truck stoned.

ROGER. You know that?

LOU. I know he's stoned all the time, and I know you let him drive the truck.

ROGER. That doesn't mean he's driving the truck stoned.

LOU. It doesn't mean he's not. I don't like that kid. Maybe I should check on him. I mean, you just handed him a lot of money and sent him out the door with it. You just handed that kid, what, forty dollars.

MEGAN. It was just twenty.

(There is a pause at that.)

I don't think he's going to run off with Roger's twenty dollars.

LOU. You don't know him, you don't know.

MEGAN. No, I don't. It just, seems like a lot of work. Stealing a twenty. It's not exactly worth the bother.

ROGER. *(Polite.)* So, how long are you here for, Megan?

MEGAN. How long am I here for?

ROGER. Yes. How long are you planning to visit?

MEGAN. He didn't tell you?

LOU. It's nobody's business.

MEGAN. It's everybody's business.

LOU. I don't see it that way.

MEGAN. It doesn't matter how you see it.

(To **ROGER**.*)* I'm not visiting, Roger. I so fucked up, I tried to kill myself? And I had nowhere to go and they couldn't let me out of the hospital unless someone said okay she can come here? So, I'm like, I don't know how long I'm here for, but it's not actually a visit. It would be great, if it were just a visit, but that's not likely.

(A pause. **ROGER** *doesn't quite know what to say.)*

LOU. It's sort of a visit.

MEGAN. Dad, I discourage you from talking about it that way. I know it's like hard and definitely too much information but you know they did tell me that I had to be very plain about my situation. So I did try to kill myself. Not that's what, I will say in my defense that I actually didn't think that's what I was doing. I did though, just keep taking pills and drinking vodka well past the point where a person should have stopped, if they didn't want to die. So I have to be able to talk about that. Even though it sucks. This is basically, sorry, Roger. But this is totally my mandate. I have to tell people things.

LOU. But not all the time.

MEGAN. Yes, all the time Dad. I have to tell everyone everything, all the time. I explained this to you.

LOU. It was an accident. She didn't really try to kill herself.

MEGAN. Is this the plant he killed?

(She looks at the plant.)

ROGER. Yes.

MEGAN. I have sympathy.

LOU. I didn't kill it. Because it's not dead.

MEGAN. They say the same thing about me.

LOU. You did that to yourself!

(A beat.)

MEGAN. I did. I surely did.

ROGER. I'm sorry you're having a hard time.

MEGAN. You and me both.

(She looks at the plant, reaches over to touch its broken leaves.)

ROGER. Don't. Don't – please.

(He takes it from her.)

LOU. I'm going to go see where that kid is with the coffee.

*(He leaves. **MEGAN** watches him. **ROGER** goes to the orchids, starts to turn them.)*

MEGAN. I embarrass him. Don't bother denying it. It wouldn't matter even if you did. The truth is the truth and if you try to get around it, it will come after you and take you down.

ROGER. Really?

MEGAN. I'm telling you, stay out of Alcoholics Anonymous. They're ruthless. This thing about the truth, it's fucking killing me. But this is the deal: You bottom out, there's always a trap door, anything can be a trap door. So you have to stick with the facts, otherwise they come back and turn into trap doors and the next thing you know. I think the theory is that if you make the truth your friend it can't just suddenly come at you and eat you alive.

ROGER. I've just never known the truth to do that.

MEGAN. Well, you're lucky then.

> (**ROGER** *has opened a canister of plant food.* **MEGAN** *picks it up and looks at it. He takes it from her.*)

ROGER. Please.

MEGAN. Sorry.

ROGER. I just have things where I want them.

MEGAN. And they stay there?

ROGER. Yes.

> (*He goes back to feeding the plant.*)

MEGAN. What is that stuff?

ROGER. It's nutrients, you know, for the soil, it keeps the plants thriving.

MEGAN. You have any for people?

ROGER. I think that's called "food." I don't know if you've heard of that.

MEGAN. I eat.

ROGER. You don't look like it.

MEGAN. Hey.

ROGER. You said I had to tell you the truth.

MEGAN. Well you're a fast learner.

> *(The door opens and **MOLLY** sticks her head in.)*

MOLLY. Hello? Are you open?

ROGER. We're not actually. We open in ten minutes.

MOLLY. I'll be fast. I just need some tulip bulbs or daffodils, whatever you have, do you have bulbs? For planting now, but they come up in the spring. Do you have any of them?

ROGER. It's a little late in the season. And we're not quite set up yet, so.

MOLLY. You think you have something, though? I wouldn't want to wait out there on the sidewalk for ten minutes just to find out that you don't have what I need.

ROGER. If you come back in ten minutes

MEGAN. You're going to make her wait on the sidewalk for ten minutes just to find out if you have some bulbs around here? She's a customer, she wants to buy something.

MOLLY. Not if it's any trouble.

MEGAN. How can it be trouble? It's a store, it's a plant store. He can sell you some bulbs.

MOLLY. Thank you.

ROGER. Let me check.

> *(He does.)*

MOLLY. This is lovely! Cozy.

MEGAN. Cozy's a good word.

MOLLY. But it is! There used to be so many little shops like this, all over. And now they're gone. I wouldn't

even know to come looking in here. It's such a funny
name. Dig. You don't actually know what kind of store
that might be.

MEGAN. *(Uninterested.)* Sure, it could be a store that
teaches you about digging.

MOLLY. That's what I mean.

MEGAN. You could buy dirt here and then go sprinkle it
around outside.

MOLLY. *(Confused.)* Oh.

MEGAN. Or maybe he could sell you a shovel.

MOLLY. I don't need a shovel.

MEGAN. You might. Someday.

MOLLY. Today I just want plants.

MEGAN. This is the place for that.

ROGER. *(Reentering.)* Well, I have the purple flag triumph,
the yokohama single, that's a yellow tulip and the orca
double, which is a nice orange.

MOLLY. Orange?

ROGER. Yeah people don't seem to respond to the whole
idea of an orange tulip. I don't know why, they're pretty.
I got that, Megan.

> *(For she is trying to write up the order for
> him.)*

MEGAN. Okay.

MOLLY. Well could you order some? Some red ones or
those striped ones, my husband likes those.

ROGER. I can't just order them by the dozen, I'd have to
order a whole crate, and people actually don't come
looking for bulbs this late in the season, so you would
have to take the whole crate.

MOLLY. Oh well. Maybe I could get them online.

ROGER. You could do that.

MEGAN. *(Annoyed.)* Don't tell her to do that. She'll go off and do it and then you lost a sale.

ROGER. She should do whatever she likes.

MEGAN. *(Still annoyed.)* Wow. Put your heart into it. Get behind it. Sell those flowers.

MOLLY. But you think these are good?

ROGER. They're reliable. They'll come up. You get them in the ground this week, I don't think you'll have a problem.

MOLLY. I'm really not the gardener at my house. My husband is ready to kill me! He asked me to pick these up at least two weeks ago. Then he said he was going to pick them up. He of course forgot that part! Orange, yellow and purple. That might be pretty.

(*She smiles at* **MEGAN.**)

MEGAN. It sounds awesome.

MOLLY. Well, I guess I'll take this then.

(**MEGAN** *takes the bulbs from her and takes them to the register.*)

ROGER. I will do this. Thank you.

(*He starts to ring them up.*)

MOLLY. Do you do a lot of gardening?

MEGAN. No.

MOLLY. So you're not here picking up bulbs then.

MEGAN. No.

MOLLY. That's a good thing! Because they're off season, so I'm told.

(**MEGAN** *attempts to smile at her, but only sort of.*)

You know, I'm sorry but you look so familiar. Have we met?

MEGAN. No.

MOLLY. Do you go to church over at Saint Cecilia's in Rockwell Township?

MEGAN. What? No.

ROGER. It's sixty-three forty-eight. You want to put it on a card?

(*He holds out the receipt.*)

MOLLY. Oh yes yes. It's not a debit card, my husband says those are just a waste of time.

ROGER. Either one is fine.

(*She finds her card and hands it to* **ROGER**, *who rings it up.*)

MOLLY. (*To* **MEGAN**.) Are you Catholic?

MEGAN. Excuse me?

ROGER. You need a bag?

MOLLY. You just look so familiar. For a while my husband and I were going to All Saints, but he didn't like the pastor over there, so we started going to St. Joseph's, but that was far, and now we drive over to St. Cecilia's so I thought if you're Catholic maybe I've seen you at any number of churches!

MEGAN. I don't go to church.

MOLLY. Wait! It was All Saints. I know it was. I remember I used to see you there with your mother and father and your brothers! You have two brothers, I remember. Your father is Hispanic. Or Latino! I never know what to call people anymore.

MEGAN. *(Rattled.)* When, when – uh, I don't.

ROGER. Here's your receipt.

MOLLY. Yes, I saw you there, it was probably three years ago now, you had your...

> (**MEGAN** *looks at her.* **MOLLY** *realizes how she knows her.* **MEGAN** *sees* **MOLLY**'s *face change.)*

MEGAN. Yep. That's me.

> (**MOLLY** *smiles, flustered.)*

MOLLY. I beg your pardon. I don't know you, do I?

MEGAN. *(Cold.)* So what are you staring at?

MOLLY. Nothing.

MEGAN. Are you judging me? You're fucking judging me. What the fuck do you think you know about me?

MOLLY. I'm sorry.

MEGAN. You don't know a fucking thing. You fucking bitch.

> (**MOLLY** *goes, fast. She almost runs into* **EVERETT**, *who holds the door open.* **LOU** *is there behind him.* **ROGER** *is left at the counter, bewildered.)*

EVERETT. Whoa! Another satisfied customer I see. Sorry that took so long. The line wasn't even that long but they only had one person at the counter.

MEGAN. We have to go.

LOU. What, we just got here.

MEGAN. WE HAVE TO GO. This is so fucking stupid. Why did you make me come down here? I told you I don't fucking want to see your fucked-up friend, I told you, I TOLD you to leave me the fuck alone, why didn't you just

LOU. *(Overlap.)* You stop it now. You stop.

EVERETT. Whoa.

MEGAN. FUCK YOU. Asshole.

> *(She blasts through the door.* **LOU** *follows her.* **EVERETT** *looks at* **ROGER**.*)*

EVERETT. Whoa.

> *(Lights change.)*

Scene Two

(The following day.)

*(****EVERETT*** *is there. He is taking a hit off a joint. Then another. He smokes alone for a long moment.* ***ROGER*** *comes out.)*

ROGER. Are you smoking a joint?

EVERETT. What? No no no no no

(He pinches it out and hides it, swift.)

ROGER. You are, you're smoking a joint. You're getting stoned. In the store.

EVERETT. I'm not getting stoned. I was just waiting for you. You called me last night, you said you needed to talk to me.

*(****ROGER*** *starts to set up the store.)*

ROGER. *(Annoyed.)* So you come over here early because you think I want to talk to you

EVERETT. I came over here early because you called me.

ROGER. So you show up at work early because I need to talk to you and you use the time to get stoned?

EVERETT. Look, okay, look. I see your point.

ROGER. You "see my point."

EVERETT. I do. But look, 'cause here's the thing. It's not illegal.

ROGER. That's not – first of all

EVERETT. It's not illegal anymore!

ROGER. It IS illegal.

EVERETT. Okay in this state maybe technically? But overall, 'cause everyone knows the way this whole situation is going.

ROGER. Stop, just stop talking.

EVERETT. Okay sure.

ROGER. Stop.

(Silence.)

EVERETT. So is there something specifically you needed to have a conversation about?

ROGER. I was just thinking it might be time for a job evaluation.

EVERETT. I love this job.

ROGER. Okay that's not

EVERETT. It's a great job. I really need this job. And I think I have a knack.

ROGER. Is that for you to say?

EVERETT. What do you mean?

ROGER. Some people would say that was for me to say. If you had a knack.

EVERETT. Don't you think that I have a knack?

ROGER. Not particularly.

EVERETT. Yeah but would you know?

ROGER. Lou thinks I should fire you.

EVERETT. Did he say that?

ROGER. Yeah, he did.

EVERETT. Does he get a vote?

ROGER. He was advising.

EVERETT. Yeah, but he doesn't know. He's just your friend, what does he know about how this place runs?

ROGER. He keeps the books.

EVERETT. Not really.

ROGER. Yes really.

EVERETT. Which I never thought was a good idea. You're like his only client right, and he does it as a favor, which isn't professional. And on top of that he wants you to fire me because it makes his job easier. Like, he has a problem because, well, because he's uptight, he thinks about money all the time, and that's not working out for him. So he's, listen, I like Lou. He's cool, I got nothing against Lou. But I do feel, I regret that he is trying to make his problem, my problem. Because I totally have a knack. And I disagree, I have to tell you that I do not agree with the proposition that other people should be telling you who you are, what you're good at. That's for you to say about yourself. Like I really do believe that people know, in their hearts, what is right. For them. Because like when I was a kid? My father, he was always, like people were always saying shit, like you should, just all stuff. Stuff that didn't matter to me.

ROGER. What does matter to you? Football? Your gamer chair? PlayStation 12?

EVERETT. They're only up to five.

ROGER. Really?

EVERETT. Okay. They matter somewhat, those things, although I realize you say all of this with disdain. But like what matters to you? These plants?

ROGER. *(Looking at him.)* Yes in fact these plants do matter to me.

EVERETT. Okay and they matter to me too. I love plants. And I love the truck, I love driving that truck.

ROGER. You're driving that truck stoned!

EVERETT. Oh now listen. The truck – that truck is a holy thing to me.

ROGER. Okay I'm told by Lou that

EVERETT. Lou doesn't know!

ROGER. *(Overlap.)* I'm told by Lou that you are doing things in the holy truck, getting stoned, driving in an unsafe manner

EVERETT. How would he know what I'm doing in the truck. I'll tell you what I'm doing in the truck. I make deliveries. I pick the guys up, we go and take care of the corporate contracts. I keep us on schedule. I do a nice job with the private customers, we have to go into people's homes to take care of their gardens and their little solariums, these are people with a lot of money who need to feel safe, I do a good job with that.

ROGER. You

EVERETT. People feel safe around me.

ROGER. I don't feel safe around you.

EVERETT. I think you do. I think I'm doing a good job here. You could use me in the shop more, even. I'm good at selling plants, at talking to people about plants.

ROGER. You're good at smoking plants.

EVERETT. I don't apologize for that. The organic world makes sense to me. And it is in fact the world we live in now.

ROGER. It is not the world I live it.

EVERETT. Your touch with the vegetation, Roger? You'd make a killing. This place could be transformed into an herbacious wonderland.

ROGER. Herbacious?

EVERETT. I have all the equipment. In my mom's basement. You got a lot more space here. We could use the shed out back. So this would be your place – Dig! – and that would be the extension. Pot.

ROGER. You know I'm not enjoying this conversation.

EVERETT. I think you are.

ROGER. I'm not.

EVERETT. Well, so okay, I accept that. But I still don't think you should fire me. Like who's going to drive the truck if you fire me?

ROGER. What is that supposed to mean?

EVERETT. It means what it means. And I say that with humility.

ROGER. You don't say anything with humility.

EVERETT. I say everything with humility.

(**ROGER** *thinks about that.*)

ROGER. Okay. I guess we understand the word "humility" in a different way.

EVERETT. That's probably true of every word.

ROGER. Oh god I actually agree with that.

EVERETT. I promise you, Roger. I hear what you're saying. In terms of your concerns, I will honor your request. Whatever my personal political convictions are around marijuana, it stays out of the shop, and out of the truck. I totally hear you. How's that for communication.

ROGER. Better.

EVERETT. Good. Because this job is important to me and I want you to be happy.

ROGER. Oh good.

(He turns his attention back to work.
EVERETT *looks out the door, makes sure no
one is coming. He goes to* **ROGER.***)*

EVERETT. I found out who she is.

(A beat.)

ROGER. Who?

EVERETT. You know who! The girl. Yesterday. The one who
flipped out like a banshee. They were talking about it
across the street.

ROGER. I advise you not to spread gossip.

EVERETT. It's not gossip! You go online, it's everywhere.

ROGER. Yes, because the internet is equally accurate.

EVERETT. She went to jail!

ROGER. Everett, I assure you, I know what happened.

EVERETT. And you're okay with it?

ROGER. You know what? I am going to fire you. You're fired.

EVERETT. What? Why?

ROGER. Because you're annoying.

EVERETT. You can't fire people for that.

ROGER. You most certainly can.

EVERETT. Look, people are talking about this all over
the street. Everybody in the Leaf and Bean saw her
come in here and now they're talking about what she
did, I'm not allowed to mention that I overheard this
conversation? You're my boss, I thought it was my job
to let you know, how people felt. I mean Lou has a lot
of nerve, complaining about me getting stoned. She's
his daughter. Adopted, I know, but let's face it. He
didn't exactly do a stellar job.

ROGER. He did fine.

EVERETT. Look. I'm just the messenger! I didn't invent the human race. Because people saw her come in here and then she screamed at a customer –

ROGER. Did you tell people that? Is that what you're doing over there, telling people things that you know nothing about?

EVERETT. I'm just saying. People know what she did. It was all over the television. Like, okay I hear you, gossip isn't good, and the internet is not fully trustworthy, but it was on television and in the newspapers. I mean… you can go on YouTube and look at the clips from the news. It was on CNN, man. It was on…like, everything.

ROGER. It was an accident.

EVERETT. She left her kid in a car seat in a locked car and he suffocated to death!

  (Beat.)

Or died of heat stroke, whatever you die of when someone does that to you.

ROGER. It's not clear, what happened.

EVERETT. It seems pretty clear. I mean, the kid is dead, isn't he?

ROGER. Yes. He is.

EVERETT. What kind of a person does that?

  *(The door opens. **MEGAN** and **LOU** are there. **EVERETT** turns, embarrassed, sort of.)*

MEGAN. Hi.

EVERETT. Yeah, hi, hi.

  (There is an awkward pause.)

MEGAN. Hey Roger.

(**LOU** *enters right behind her.*)

Dad, do you mind giving me a little privacy?

LOU. You're not going to run away?

(*There is a sad pause.*)

MEGAN. No I'm not going to run away.

(*He leaves.* **EVERETT**, **ROGER** *and* **MEGAN**.)

I uh I wanted to come by because, Roger, I…owe you an apology.

(*She looks at* **EVERETT**, *then, annoyed.*)

Aren't you going to leave?

EVERETT. You owe me an apology too, don't you?

MEGAN. I'm sorry.

EVERETT. Okay.

(*Then.*)

Is that it?

MEGAN. Yes could Roger and I have some privacy please?

EVERETT. Sure, of course. I'll just go across the street. Get some coffee. See what's going on over there.

(*He goes.*)

ROGER. You don't have to apologize.

MEGAN. I do actually. They really are just ruthless over there at A.A. So I apologize. It was inappropriate for me to get so upset about that woman. I mean this is your shop and you live here and that was bad, I shouldn't have lost my temper.

ROGER. She was...

MEGAN. No no no, Don't let me off. I was bad. So I apologize.

ROGER. I accept your apology.

MEGAN. Thanks.

(She stands there.)

ROGER. Is there more?

MEGAN. I need a job.

ROGER. Oh.

MEGAN. Not like a normal job. Like you wouldn't have to pay me.

ROGER. I just...

MEGAN. I could just help clean and stuff. Like you could keep me in the back. I wouldn't need to talk to people.

ROGER. Well.

MEGAN. Okay, sure.

ROGER. It's just

MEGAN. No I get it. I totally get it.

ROGER. It's just more complicated than it looks.

MEGAN. But you wouldn't have to pay me. I wouldn't even have to be an intern. I could be a helper. And I wouldn't talk to the customers.

(She reaches out to touch a plant leaf.)

I could help you.

ROGER. Please, that –

(He tries to take it from her. She holds it back.)

MEGAN. What.

ROGER. That's actually not, it's a little delicate.

MEGAN. It doesn't look delicate.

ROGER. Well, it's very, it needs to be re-potted so please don't can you –

(He takes it from her.)

MEGAN. Okay. Okay. I can re-pot it.

ROGER. No you can't.

MEGAN. You could teach me.

ROGER. It's not a good time. I'm sorry.

(She nods. After a moment.)

MEGAN. Why does it need to be re-potted?

ROGER. It's pot-bound.

MEGAN. What's pot-bound?

ROGER. It's too healthy, it just kept growing. It's something that happens to plants. The roots eat up everything around them. They take in the light and the soil and the air and the leaves, through photosynthesis – you know about photosynthesis?

MEGAN. I've heard of it.

ROGER. It's a series of chemical reactions, requiring carbon dioxide and water, which converts light energy into the chemical energy of sugars. The leaf releases oxygen, after moving electrons and making sugars out of the CO2, and then that goes down into the roots, while the roots are carrying water up to the leaf to continue the process.

MEGAN. Ohhhh.

ROGER. Right, so with a healthy plant this is a two-way process, obviously, and the leaves grow but they have space

MEGAN. Yes I see that.

ROGER. But for the roots, in the pots, they run out of space. The soil breaks down and then the roots are pressing against the sides of the pot, the pot is no longer big enough, this is actually a relatively simple concept. It's like a child growing out of his clothes.

> *(He stops. She looks at him.)*

MEGAN. It's okay.

ROGER. I know.

MEGAN. Kids outgrow their clothes.

ROGER. *(Uncomfortable.)* Of course you have to be careful not to diagnose this too recklessly as most house plants actually thrive best in pots which appear to the beginner to be too small for the amount of leaf and stem, also some plants will only flower in this condition and others, say Bromeliads, should never need re-potting.

> *(Then.)*

Those that do, need re-potting, the stem and leaf growth slows, of course. Roots grow through the drainage hole. There may be a matted mass of roots visible on the outside, and not much soil on the inside.

MEGAN. *(Simple.)* So this plant's in trouble, and needs to be in a bigger pot. I assume you have bigger pots around here somewhere.

ROGER. Yes, in the back.

> *(She takes the plant and heads back to the*
> *back of the shop, goes out the back door.*
> ***ROGER*** *stands alone for a moment, adrift.*
> ***LOU*** *comes in.)*

LOU. Where'd she go.

ROGER. Ahhh.

(He goes to mess with his plants.)

LOU. I'm not kidding, where'd she go? You can't just let her go places. They were clear. She's…

ROGER. She's out back, repotting a hydrangea.

LOU. I don't think she should be doing that.

ROGER. I don't think she should either.

LOU. Well, why did you tell her to do it.

ROGER. I didn't tell her. She just – took it. She says she needs a job.

LOU. You're giving her a job?

ROGER. I am not giving her a job. Absolutely not.

LOU. Because I don't want her working here.

ROGER. Are you listening to me?

LOU. You saw what happened, yesterday, that was just yesterday, that woman

ROGER. That woman was rude.

LOU. So there are rude people in the world and we all learn to deal with that fact, we don't – curse them – to their faces –

ROGER. Look. I don't blame her for losing her temper with that woman. She's been through a hard time.

LOU. Don't talk to me about what she's been through. She killed her own kid. That beautiful boy. I mean she was always a screw-up but never in a million years would anyone have believed that she could do something so grotesque. I should never have let her come home.

ROGER. Did you have a choice?

LOU. I did have a choice, yes. She's a grown woman. She did what she did, she's not my responsibility.

ROGER. Well, she's not mine either.

LOU. That's what I'm saying! She is my child. She was only six when I came into the picture and I said that, to Ginny, when we got married, I will raise her as my child. I never thought of her as "adopted." When people would say oh you adopted her when she was a little girl? I wanted to hit them. She is my daughter. From the moment I met her, I loved this girl. You don't expect, you don't expect…

ROGER. I know I know.

LOU. Maybe it was too, maybe I maybe I

ROGER. No no come on.

LOU. I'm not kidding, you just wonder what you could have done more, and they say that kids who are adopted maybe don't feel, there's a hole in them. The boys don't have it! Maybe it really made a difference, the biology thing. But I treated them all the same, I swear I did. When people said, "So the boys are yours biologically but she's your adopted daughter, right?" I said they're all my kids!

ROGER. You were a terrific father. You are a terrific father.

(*A terrible silence.*)

She was such a cute little thing.

LOU. That's the past.

ROGER. You can't get away from the past. Everyone says, forget the past, live in the present. I have yet to see anyone do it.

LOU. Some days I wish she had, the night she took all those pills? I just wish…

ROGER. You don't wish that. Come on. You don't wish that.

LOU. Listen. I need you to be with me on this.

ROGER. What does that mean?

LOU. When I tell her she has to, you know, find a different place to live.

ROGER. Are you going to do that?

LOU. I don't want you coming back and giving her a job.

ROGER. I didn't say I was giving her a job. What is the matter with you. All I said was she asked, she says she needs a job.

LOU. Yeah but not here.

> *(This annoys **ROGER**, mostly because he doesn't like being told things.)*

ROGER. Why not here?

LOU. It's pity. You don't need another person to help you, this is just pity.

ROGER. Look there are worse reasons out there to give a person a job.

LOU. I don't like people doing things for me out of pity.

ROGER. I'm not doing it for either of you.

LOU. She doesn't deserve your pity.

ROGER. Oh my god. Pity is not

LOU. Okay here we go.

ROGER. What do you mean, "here we go."

LOU. She doesn't want your pity.

ROGER. Could we use a different word? Pity is a bad word, I don't know why but

LOU. She doesn't take responsibility.

ROGER. She tried to kill herself! How much responsibility do you want her to take?

LOU. You're my friend. This whole thing is hard. She's living in my house. Which I don't know if I'm even going to be able to keep anymore, you know I had to take out a second mortgage because of all her legal fees. You know that. And that's not even, that's not the point. That's not... I can't stop seeing that little boy. What a sweet kid. And I'm not gonna talk to her about it. Forget it. Forget it.

 (This is hard for him to say, and hard for **ROGER** *to hear.)*

ROGER. The doctors tell you

LOU. I don't know what they told me. But let me tell you, it's not like when Ginny got sick. Take her in for her chemo. Bring her home, make her scrambled eggs and toast. Buy her a wig when her hair falls out. This, how do you take care of this? She doesn't get out of bed in the morning. I have to go in there and say, are you getting up?

ROGER. Well – maybe that's why she asked for a job.

LOU. Not here! I'm not kidding. What if she did something? What if she stole, or started a fire.

ROGER. You can't start a fire in a plant store, plants don't burn.

LOU. Don't make a joke. This isn't a joke. You could lose everything and then I wouldn't be able to look at you. I don't want you in the middle of this. She's already cost me enough. I said I'd take her in, help her get back on her feet, both her brothers refuse to visit while she's here. Then the way she acts. People don't act like that. You'll see, you invite her in here, into your shop, you don't know what's going to happen. You still see her as a little girl. I'm telling you she's not a little girl anymore.

 (A beat.)

ROGER. *(Pissed.)* I am not in the middle of this. You show up here, how long have we been friends? You think I don't know what you're doing? This is you, this is just you all over. As soon as something goes wrong, you think

LOU. What do I think

ROGER. You brought her here! To my shop. Where everything, this is how I want things. I worked hard my whole life, making things the way I want them. And then you you you

LOU. What? I what?

ROGER. Why did you bring her here?

> *(They stare at each other. Both are pissed.* **MEGAN** *enters, carrying the hydrangea. It is in a bigger pot.)*

MEGAN. I did it! I repotted the hydrangea. I think it's going to do better in this pot. I think it looks better in this pot. That old pot was pretty old and crusty. I think it's going to really appreciate this pot.

> *(She sets it down, looks at it. Silence.)*

ROGER. Yeah, the roots are happier, certainly.

MEGAN. Okay. What else can I re-pot?

> *(A beat.)*

ROGER. The philodendron is...

MEGAN. Which one, this one?

ROGER. Yes.

> *(She carries it off. Blackout.)*

Scene Three

*(Two weeks later. **ROGER** has a large shrub
in the middle of the shop. It's in a giant
pot. **EVERETT** is at the counter, watching, as
ROGER explains pruning to **MEGAN**.)*

ROGER. All right, it has to be said before we even start,
that there is nothing more traumatic than pruning.
Whether it's pinch pruning where you take your
fingernails and pinch out the growth at the end to full
take out your shears and prune it down to the ground
and let it rejuvenate, pruning is both delicate and
devastating and you cannot take it lightly.

MEGAN. What do you mean down to the ground?

ROGER. That means just what it means. I've seen trees
after major prunings just look like stumps. When
you have to do something like that it's really extreme,
that's something you do to get rid of disease or serious
damage, and you don't know if anything's coming back
at all when you have to take a tree down that far. And
then the next thing you know, there are little shoots
that come up the next year. But that's drastic. Most of
the time you want to do something more considered,
which is why, sorry, I'm ahead of myself. Let's start with
pinch pruning.

*(**EVERETT** shakes his head at this, but **MEGAN**
is paying attention, as **ROGER** demonstrates.)*

Pinch pruning is largely a cosmetic thing, you just want
to make the plant fuller, keep it from getting leggy. It's
minor and sometimes even, if you're passing by and
you see something that's stretching out a little, you can
just reach over and take care of it. It's like petting a dog,
you're just letting the plant know you care about it, like
ruffling its fur. Or you might find that you need to do

a little more than that. But generally pinch pruning is light, simple, like that.

> *(He picks a little piece of the plant off it, gives it to her to look at. She does while he goes to the counter and fetches a set of pruning shears.)*

And then there's maintenance pruning, keep things healthy, so you use the shears to go further down into the branches and remove stuff that's getting too thinned out, too tall. You can prune for shape, like a topiary, if you want your bush to look like a rabbit, say. But largely you do this for the deep health of the plant.

Conventional wisdom is that with big shrubs you remove a third of the oldest growth every year after they flower which helps them open up, which allows air circulation and new growth, allows them to flourish. And then sometimes there's just terminal pruning. Which means digging a plant out of the ground and tossing it into the dumpster. Because no matter what you did it didn't work, it just, nothing worked. There was nothing you could do.

> *(He thinks about that.)*

Oh there's root pruning as well. Which is frankly pretty advanced, although you use the same instruments. Root pruning involves cutting the roots all the way around so you're stimulating more growth in the root ball, or conversely, if you want to limit the size, like a bonzai tree, you go at the roots.

MEGAN. So wait.

ROGER. *(Agreeing.)* I know it seems like a contradiction! But it's true, you do both things with root pruning, it stimulates growth and it inhibits growth. You're not going to have to worry about that for a while. Today we're just looking at pinch pruning and maintenance pruning. So I want you to come over here and carefully – all of this honestly has to be done with the utmost, going after a plant and removing part of it is both loving and dangerous. You must never forget that everything you do is to give the plant a fuller foliage and a fuller life, but in the moment of pruning, it is not going to fully understand that. I like to stand and not talk to the plant for a moment, that would be crazy, but just touch it lightly, let it know you're here, you have its best interest at heart, you have to be at peace yourself, so that you can reassure it.

> (**MEGAN** *does this. She and* **ROGER** *stand by the plant.* **EVERETT** *jumps off the counter, finally.*)

EVERETT. Okay but I'm just not sure why we're going through this.

ROGER. A lot of the fall maintenance contracts are going to require substantial pruning

EVERETT. Yeah, I am on top of it. I mean, the pruning thing I got covered.

ROGER. There's always room.

EVERETT. Room for what? Are you sending her out in the truck now? Because if she's coming out in the truck, there's going to need to be some discussion about that.

ROGER. Discussion, there's no discussion.

EVERETT. I think there should be.

ROGER. Didn't I fire you at some point?

EVERETT. You can't fire me because you need me in charge of the truck. And my point is here, you run this shop, that's your business. But I run the truck.

ROGER. You don't run the truck. You drive the truck. You run the truck, for me.

EVERETT. Come on, man. You can't say I don't run that truck.

ROGER. I can say it because I own the truck. Why do I even talk to you?

EVERETT. Because you know that I care about you and I care about this shop, Roger! I'm saying this because I love you, man!

ROGER. Oh my god.

EVERETT. Seriously. I am committed to you and this shop. I love this place, to the bottom of my heart, you can't doubt that. If you doubted that I would not still be working here! You think I don't know that?

MEGAN. It's okay. I don't want to go in the truck.

(To **EVERETT.***)* I don't want to be in your stupid truck.

EVERETT. Good.

MEGAN. I'm in A.A. You know, I'm not allowed to get high. So I can't be in the truck. It's like a rule of A.A., you have to stay out of bars. And trucks that are like stepping inside a giant vaporizor. You have to stay out of them, too.

EVERETT. Yeah that's hilarious.

MEGAN. I'm so pleased to amuse you.

EVERETT. I do not get high in the truck.

MEGAN. That truck is a weedmobile.

EVERETT. That's a lie.

MEGAN. I wouldn't get in that truck if you paid me.

EVERETT. I'm sorry, but – okay I'm just going to say it. It is a little amazing to be accused of doing something illegal by someone who –

MEGAN. *(Overlap.)* Listen you fucking asshole if you ever knew a fucking thing

ROGER. *(Loud.)* STOP. Stop!

EVERETT. Sorry, but there's like an elephant in the room here. She is only here because she killed her own kid and then she wrecked her life and you're a totally nice man, Roger, you think you can help a person like that but Roger, a person like that is beyond help. As I think everybody else can see, except you. And no one comes in here anymore, in case you haven't noticed. If you ask me the only reason you are thinking about putting her on the truck is because there's nothing for her to DO here because since she showed up people avoid this place like the plague. You go over to the Leaf and Bean for a coffee and the whole place goes silent! So I'm carrying the whole operation now, with the delivery schedule and the maintenance projects but if she gets involved in that there's no telling what will happen. The whole place could come down.

   (A beat.)

ROGER. You're fired.

EVERETT. I'm serious.

ROGER. So am I, you're fired. You don't work here anymore.

EVERETT. You can't fire me.

ROGER. You're fired! Get out of here. You're fired. YOU'RE FIRED.

EVERETT. Okay fine this place is done anyway. And you may not like to hear it but it is the truth, it's because of her.

   *(**ROGER** raises the pruning shears as if he's going to attack him. **EVERETT** splits, fast. After a moment, **MEGAN** comes up and takes the pruning shears from him.)*

MEGAN. Good bye and good bye. What a waste of time that idiot turned out to be. And I have to tell you, Roger, all protests to the contrary, he was getting stoned in that truck.

ROGER. I'm aware.

MEGAN. I knew guys like that in rehab. They're so sure, they're so completely fucked up and yet utterly convinced that every word out of their mouths is fucking gold. And they got to tell you, everything that you're doing wrong. I hate that guy. I mean, it's totally unsafe having a person like that drive a truck.

ROGER. This is my shop.

MEGAN. *(Startled.)* I know.

ROGER. Why is everyone always telling me what to do in my shop? This is ridiculous. I have things the way I like them. And then everyone comes in and changes everything and tells me that I don't know what I know. What are you doing here?

MEGAN. You hired me.

ROGER. I didn't! You came in here and said hire me and I said no. Didn't I say no? Why are you still here?

MEGAN. Do you want me to go?

ROGER. Yes, I want you to go. I'm very unhappy. I'm unhappy with Everett, I'm unhappy with your father, and I'm unhappy with you. And don't get me wrong, I like you, when you were a little girl, you were very charming and I felt real fondness for you and I'm sorry about all the trouble that has befallen you. But I can't have it under my roof.

(*A beat.*)

MEGAN. Can I just make one observation?

ROGER. No.

MEGAN. I'm the newcomer here. I've only been here for like, minutes into the big picture. If your life is out of control I'm not the person who made it out of control.

ROGER. Is that another brilliant observation you learned at A.A.?

MEGAN. Look. Did you or did you not want to fire that guy?

ROGER. I need someone to drive the truck!

MEGAN. I could drive it.

ROGER. No. No one wants to see you, in a car. I'm sorry but that's true. And I can't afford, it's true, people don't come in here. Not because you're here, but they don't come. It's a bad location. That coffee shop. Everyone said it would anchor the neighborhood but it didn't do that, it just turned into a place for people to go and gossip. It's toxic. People go there, they say terrible things about other people and then they go away. And they don't come over here and buy anything. Nothing. They shop down at the Target. They'd rather walk six blocks to Target to buy a trowel. Or some plant food. Or a plant.

MEGAN. They sell plants at Target?

ROGER. *(Bitter.)* They sell everything at Target. And I don't care. I own my own building, and I own my own shop, and no one can kick me out, and I have things the way I like them. And that is what I want. And this extra trouble is more than I can have.

MEGAN. Can I make another observation?

ROGER. No.

> *(The door opens behind them.* **MOLLY** *is there.)*

MOLLY. Helloooo. Excuse me. Are you open?

ROGER. We're not actually.

MOLLY. The door's open. It's only four! It says on the door you don't close till six.

ROGER. Well, we're closed.

MEGAN. *(Getting it together.)* No we're not, we're open. Can I help you?

MOLLY. I hope so. I was in here, a couple weeks ago, buying tulip bulbs, do you remember?

(A beat.)

MEGAN. I remember. And, uh, I'm glad you came back in, because I need to apologize for that. I was out of line. I'm sorry. It was inappropriate, losing my temper like that. I'm sorry.

(A beat.)

MOLLY. I forgive you.

MEGAN. You forgive me?

MOLLY. Yes.

MEGAN. You know you – you don't actually need to forgive me. You just need to accept the apology.

*(**MOLLY** steps forward, anxious, blurting.)*

MOLLY. I was very upset about what happened. Because of course I recognized you, from when there was so much news about what happened, in the newspaper. But that was a little while ago so I didn't put it together right away, and when I realized who you were, I just didn't know what to say. Because I remember watching your trial on television and thinking what a terrible person you must be, to do that to your own child. Not that you even did anything, you just forgot him and left that poor little boy in the car to die like that, I had just so many feelings of rage toward you, so that when I saw you here, it was such a shock.

*(She pauses. **MEGAN** thinks about how to respond to that, then **MOLLY** continues.)*

MOLLY. And then when you just blew up like that I was already in a space of shock and fear and then you suddenly screamed curse words at me so I felt that you were some kind of truly hideous monster, just a monster, and I had no feelings of forgiveness in my heart toward you. Why would I, you were someone who murdered your own child and then you were clearly just filled with rage, it was truly frightening.

MEGAN. *(Stunned.)* Okay.

MOLLY. But then I went to church and I prayed to Jesus to ask him to help me forgive you for what you'd done. And I have to tell you, I heard nothing. Jesus said nothing to me, that might allow me to open my heart to you. But then I went to my prayer group and I told them everything. I was heartbroken and full of fear. And I confess full of anger too, toward you. And they told me –

    (A beat.)

They told me I needed to forgive you.

    *(She starts to sob. **MEGAN** looks at her.)*

And I said I didn't understand that. But they said you were a lost lamb, and that whether or not you even knew to ask for it, you needed forgiveness.

    *(She takes **MEGAN**'s hand. Then, after a moment, she hugs her. **MEGAN** just stands there. **MOLLY** pulls back and smiles at her.)*

And they were right! Because the first thing you did, when I came through the door, was ask for my forgiveness. So Jesus did speak to me, after all. He spoke to me through my prayer group, and now he is speaking to you.

    (She wipes her eyes.)

I can't have a baby myself. My husband and I, we tried so hard! Too much information I know! But I think that's why my heart was so hardened toward you. I blamed you. You had that beautiful child and you just threw him away. And I blamed God. It makes no sense but it's true. Okay too much information! But I do. I forgive you.

(There is a terrible pause at this.)

MEGAN. Well, thank you.

MOLLY. And Jesus forgives you too. And if you wanted to come join our prayer group, I think people would be really happy to have you.

(A beat.)

MEGAN. So it's like meetings? Because I already have quite a few meetings on my plate.

MOLLY. Well, just think about it. I know it's not for everyone. But you never know. Sometimes grace, and mercy, really do just – appear.

> *(She smiles at **ROGER**, and goes. After a moment **MEGAN** cuts another branch off the shrub, with some ferocity. Then another branch. **ROGER** comes over to her and gently puts his hand on hers, takes the pruning shears away from her.)*

MEGAN. I'm sorry.

ROGER. It's okay.

> *(**MEGAN** puts her hand on the table for a moment, to steady herself. **ROGER** puts his arm out to her shoulder, to comfort her.)*

(Blackout.)

Scene Four

> (**MEGAN** *and* **ROGER** *working.* **ROGER** *is spraying a giant tree.* **MEGAN** *is moving orchids from the window to the counter, where she is putting them in large baskets.)*

ROGER. What are you doing.

MEGAN. They're getting too much light in the window.

ROGER. They're orchids, they can't get too much light.

MEGAN. Yeah but if you have them over here by the cash register, people might feel like buying them more.

ROGER. Put them back in the window.

MEGAN. Seriously people do this. I've been in stores. You're in the line at the checkout and then you see something right there by the computer that you think you might want and so you buy it, on the spot.

ROGER. That's ridiculous.

MEGAN. Ridiculous or not, it works. People are idiots, Roger, haven't you noticed this? It's called a snap purchase.

ROGER. You made that up.

MEGAN. No, I think that's what they call it. Snap judgement. Snap purchase. It's something like that.

ROGER. Those orchids cost fifty some odd dollars. No one makes a snap purchase of a fifty-dollar orchid.

MEGAN. *(Reading the tag.)* This one costs a hundred and fifty.

ROGER. No it doesn't.

MEGAN. It's very rare.

ROGER. It's not.

MEGAN. It absolutely is. And the pot is gorgeous.

(She is writing a new tag.)

ROGER. You can't charge that much for a garden variety orchid.

MEGAN. There's no such thing as a garden variety orchid. Orchids are special. Look at this, it looks like an angel.

ROGER. An angel.

MEGAN. It has wings, and a heart. I'd pay a hundred and fifty dollars for this.

ROGER. Then you'd be paying three times what it's worth.

MEGAN. Why are you always so cranky.

ROGER. I'm not cranky.

MEGAN. You're pretty fucking cranky most of the time. And it seems to me that a person who gets to hang out with plants all day should be more

ROGER. More what, serene? Like hanging around plants makes you one with the universe of growing things and so you should be serene and grateful and full of light?

MEGAN. I don't know about full of light but "serene and grateful" sounds

ROGER. *(Annoyed.)* I am serene and grateful. You should see me when I'm not around plants.

MEGAN. Are you ever not around plants?

ROGER. No.

MEGAN. How long have you been doing this, anyway?

ROGER. I'm sorry, what?

MEGAN. Were you born this way?

ROGER. I was born the way everyone else was born.

MEGAN. When did you get your first plant?

ROGER. My "first plant"?

MEGAN. I'm just making conversation.

ROGER. My mother had a garden.

MEGAN. And you helped her?

ROGER. She didn't really know what she was doing. It was just like this block of dirt alongside our house. We would put carrot seeds in there and water them. String beans. Radishes. Easy stuff.

MEGAN. Did you eat them?

ROGER. They didn't really grow all that well. It was too hot, the soil was like a brick of solid – she would water and water that little patch of dirt and it was always like a rock. It was like the water just didn't know how to help. It couldn't stick around long enough to do anything useful.

 (A beat.)

MEGAN. That's a sad story.

ROGER. It was a sad garden. I kept saying to her when are the plants coming and she would just tell me it takes time but I knew something was wrong. I spent so much time thinking about those seeds, and worrying about them. I finally went out and dug them up, just to see what was going on down there in the ground. Most of them hadn't done anything, they were just still seeds. There were one or two which had started to germinate. But the little sprouts didn't have anywhere to go. They just were stuck down there. Then at some point I thought, there's got to be an easier way to do this. So I put some plants in my bedroom.

MEGAN. You put them in your bedroom?

ROGER. In pots, on the windowsill.

MEGAN. That was smart.

ROGER. I hardly invented it.

MEGAN. But you couldn't grow a carrot in a pot.

ROGER. No no, I was more interested in house plants. You know, the pretty ones. Coleus. Ivy. I had some cacti, because I knew they'd be hard to kill. And then I got a little more adventurous. One time I grew a pumpkin from a pumpkin seed, that was exciting. It never flowered but it did come up. Later on when I knew a little more I had some different strains of ivy, a couple of larger plants, I've always had a soft spot for a philodendron, they're so strong.

MEGAN. How old were you when you started this jungle in your bedroom?

ROGER. It wasn't a jungle.

MEGAN. It sounds like a jungle.

ROGER. A certain part of my bedroom was

MEGAN. It sounds like it.

ROGER. I was about nine or ten.

(A beat.)

MEGAN. You did it for your mom? You were a little boy, and you did all this for your mom?

(She is a little rocky, suddenly.)

ROGER. No. No! On the contrary. On the contrary.

(But he doesn't know what else to say. She is starting to cry, but she gets it together.)

MEGAN. Well, you clearly have a knack. I wish I had a knack for something.

ROGER. You're pretty good at this.

MEGAN. I'm not.

ROGER. You have a nice touch. It just takes time. I've been doing this, what, forty years now.

MEGAN. So if I did it for forty years you think I'd be as good as you?

ROGER. It's possible. Not probable. But possible.

(*He goes to the counter, starts to rearrange what she's rearranged.*)

MEGAN. Leave that alone, it looks better like that.

ROGER. There's no room.

MEGAN. Yeah but

ROGER. It's my store.

(*He moves the orchid back.*)

MEGAN. Absolutely. This is the way we do things at "Dig." Dig. Dig.

ROGER. What?

MEGAN. Well, you have to admit, it's a funny name for a store.

ROGER. I don't admit that.

MEGAN. There are million better ideas out there. Plant. Leaf. Prune.

ROGER. "Prune" sounds like a health food store.

MEGAN. (*Continuing her line of thought.*) Petal. Blossom. Seed.

ROGER. You may pretend I did not ask.

(*They keep working.*)

MEGAN. So once you started having plants you always had plants?

ROGER. I'm not sure what you mean.

MEGAN. That jungle in your bedroom.

ROGER. Yes?

MEGAN. Is it still there? I mean, like in high school or college, did you still have a jungle in your bedroom?

ROGER. It was hardly a jungle.

MEGAN. I just never dated anybody who had a bunch of plants in his bedroom. Like, what did girls say, when you brought them over? Did they like it? Or boys, I mean? Girls or boys? Whoever came over to your bedroom, I mean?

(He looks at her, annoyed now.)

Is that none of my business?

ROGER. No, it's none of your business.

MEGAN. You know my business. Everyone in America knows my business.

(A beat.)

ROGER. I have not pried.

MEGAN. No, I know. I'll tell you things if you want, though. I'm supposed to talk about it. They think if I talk about it I won't kill myself. I'm not sure why anybody cares if I kill myself. But the fact is, there's all this noise in my head and if I don't say it out loud it just sits in there and then I'm just alone with it and it gets to be too much and most of it if you just take it one little bit at a time, it's actually not so bad.

(A beat.)

He liked bees. The ones with the big yellow and black stripes, bumblebees. He went as a bumblebee to Halloween last year. Two years ago. Sorry. It was actually…

> *(Then.)*

MEGAN. I think about that, when I come here. Being around all these plants. Bees and plants. He would have had a lot of fun here.

> *(A beat.)*

(Dry.) I still feel like killing myself. I don't know why they think talking about it is going to solve that bit.

ROGER. Do they really think that?

MEGAN. It's hard to say. I think it's sort of like losing weight. Nobody knows what really works but they still have a bunch of rules about it. Honestly I think it makes everyone feel more in control, when in fact no one's in control.

ROGER. I'm in control.

MEGAN. Are you?

ROGER. Well, I was until you showed up.

> *(He is fussing around his plants.* **MEGAN** *considers him.)*

MEGAN. Are you a virgin?

ROGER. What?

MEGAN. Are you a virgin, you act like a virgin.

ROGER. I do not act like a virgin.

MEGAN. Yes you do.

ROGER. How do virgins act?

MEGAN. They act like you.

ROGER. Well, I am not a virgin.

MEGAN. Who did you have sex with?

ROGER. I don't have to tell you that.

MEGAN. I tell you everything. And there's nobody here, except for the plants.

ROGER. It's private.

MEGAN. Who am I going to tell?

ROGER. Why do you want to know?

MEGAN. It wasn't a plant, was it?

ROGER. What? No!

MEGAN. Because that wouldn't count.

ROGER. That is disgusting.

MEGAN. Well, who was it? Was it fun? Was it nice?

ROGER. It was fine.

MEGAN. Where was it? Was it in your bedroom? Was it in a jungle? Were you surrounded by plants?

ROGER. I am not talking about this!

MEGAN. Why not? It sounds fantastic. To have sex surrounded by plants, watching you and cheering you on.

ROGER. They don't have any eyes.

MEGAN. Do you want to do it?

ROGER. What?

MEGAN. Come on. No one comes in here. No one will know.

ROGER. You mean –

MEGAN. Yeah, with me. That's what I mean.

ROGER. What? No.

MEGAN. You're not interested in having sex with me?

ROGER. No! I am not interested in having sex with you.

MEGAN. Why not? I'm attractive.

ROGER. You are the daughter of my oldest friend.

MEGAN. That's why you should do it! Come on. I'm of age. I'm thirty-six years old. You wouldn't exactly be taking advantage of me. I mean, I'm the one standing here begging for it.

ROGER. I think I would be taking advantage of you.

MEGAN. But you wouldn't be.

ROGER. That's not up to you to say.

MEGAN. I think you are a virgin.

ROGER. I'm not a virgin.

MEGAN. I don't really care if you are, or not. That's not why I asked.

ROGER. We shouldn't be talking about this.

MEGAN. Why not?

(She goes to him, puts her arm on his shoulder.)

ROGER. *(A step back.)* You don't know what you're doing.

MEGAN. I do know what I'm doing. I've had sex lots of times, and with lots of different men, and I'd like to have sex with you.

ROGER. That wouldn't be appropriate.

MEGAN. Why not?

ROGER. I'm your boss.

MEGAN. You don't pay me.

ROGER. I was thinking I'd pay you.

MEGAN. I'd rather have sex.

ROGER. Which is even more inappropriate.

MEGAN. I'm not interested in appropriate.

ROGER. Well, I am.

MEGAN. You think I'm not attracted to you? You think I'm just doing this because I'm crazy. Because I have no boundaries anymore? Because I'm only barely human, now?

ROGER. I don't know why you would be doing it.

MEGAN. I didn't lose my mind. I lost everything else. I'm not kidding. I hadn't thought about it before just like right now? But this seems like a really good idea to me. These plants think it's a good idea, too.

ROGER. You don't know anything about plants.

MEGAN. I know what you've taught me. This idea, it's germinating. It's sprouting. It's not stuck underground. It's…

(She kisses him. He tries to back away. But then he doesn't.)

Roger. Think of me as a plant.

(He looks at her, angry. It is not clear what he is going to do. Blackout.)

ACT TWO

(Two weeks later. The store is in bloom.)

*(***ROGER*** is at the counter, reading a catalogue.
LOU, with two cups of coffee, looks about.)*

LOU. Place looks great.

ROGER. Thanks.

LOU. Lot of color. More of the plants with the what do you
call them.

ROGER. Flowers?

LOU. No I know that's what you call them, I just thought
there was maybe a more technical term.

ROGER. No that's the term.

LOU. So you're expanding your stock.

ROGER. Turns out there's more of a market for flowering
plants.

LOU. In this neighborhood?

ROGER. It's a good location. There's foot traffic.

LOU. Not really.

*(***ROGER*** goes to the computer.)*

What are you doing?

ROGER. Just putting an order in.

LOU. You hate computers.

ROGER. I don't hate computers.

LOU. You do. That's why I do your books for you every year. You can't figure the damn thing out.

ROGER. Well. Megan showed me a few things. It's not as incomprehensible as I thought.

(**LOU** *looks around.*)

LOU. So. Megan's helping you with all this.

ROGER. Yeah, she's, you know, she's really got a knack. And she's a hard worker.

LOU.   News to me. But god knows she's never home anymore. She's here all the time. So she tells me.

(**ROGER** *nods.*)

ROGER. Well, she's doing a good job.

LOU. I know I've been a little scarce lately. And that's not my doing. I mean, I know you felt, before, that I was maybe dumping my problem on you.

ROGER. I didn't

LOU. No, it's what you said. And I'm just reminding you that I refuted that. I said don't hire her.

ROGER. She's doing a good job.

LOU. She informed me that she needed her space. This is her space now. My version of this space no longer exists. I told you this would happen. She'd come in, take over, can't say I didn't warn you.

(**ROGER** *nods, keeps working.* **LOU** *looks around, dissatisfied that he's not getting any pushback on this. He considers the flowers.*)

I just didn't think you went in for this stuff.

ROGER. What do you mean, "stuff." It's plants.

LOU. Just, it's colorful. I didn't think you went in for that.

ROGER. *(Deflecting.)* I agree, I agree, I haven't been as curious about the angiosperm in all its permutations as I might have been. The whole, the reason, of course, that the plant even does this –

LOU. The angio what?

ROGER. The flower.

LOU. I asked, didn't I ask the fancy name?

ROGER. *(Ignoring that.)* The evolution of the earliest angiosperm took place one hundred and forty million years ago and frankly the planet has never recovered. They're the dominant life force on the whole earth.

LOU. The dominant life force? Flowers?

ROGER. They have been insanely successful at mutating and replicating. They didn't exist and now they're everywhere. Kind of like people.

LOU. All I'm saying, you never had them around. One or two orchids in the window, but this other stuff, you didn't sell this stuff.

ROGER. I confess I was a little bit of a snob about the angiosperm, I found them trivial, too eager to please, canine even in their determination to attract so much attention. And I got to be honest for the longest time I found their whole obsession with their own reproductive system to be a little – never mind.

LOU. No, I'm interested.

ROGER. Well, it alternates between a diploid sporophyte generation, and a haploid gametophyte generation. The whole thing always struck me as too changeable. I always thought, those blooms are a problem, people are out there killing plants all over the place so that they can have fresh cut flowers. And then they die and they throw them away and go out and get some more. It's so wasteful. But there are so many varieties of indoor blooming plants. They're not as easy to care for as non-blooming varietals, it does take horticultural skill but people can be taught. They can be taught. And they have such beautiful names. The Italian Bellflower. That one in the corner is a Peace Lily. This one here is a Viola, isn't that a pretty little flower? The Viola. That's, I just think that's...lovely.

LOU. I think you've lost your mind.

ROGER. No doubt you're right.

*(The front door opens. **EVERETT** is there, carrying a couple of cups of coffee.)*

EVERETT. Hey, Roger.

ROGER. Everett.

EVERETT. I bumped into Megan over at the Leaf and Bean, she needed a hand.

*(**MEGAN** is right behind her, carrying a giant plant.)*

MEGAN. Hey Roger get a load of this.

ROGER. Wow.

MEGAN. Right?

LOU. What's that, another dead plant?

MEGAN. *(Bristling.)* Dad, hi.

LOU. Thing's a mess.

MEGAN. They had it over in the corner at the Leaf and Bean, I always thought it was fake but then I thought you know that fake plant is not looking so hot, and of course it's not fake at all and nobody has been watering it over there. So I said to the guy behind the counter, what is up with you fucking clowns, this corn plant is just dying in the corner over here doesn't anybody fucking think of watering it? And he said you know, nobody's really looking out for it and if I wanted it I should take it.

EVERETT. Yeah I've noticed that plant myself, there in the corner for a while. I mean, I did know it was a real plant, I wasn't confused about that part. But definitely, you definitely noticed that it needed more of a hands-on approach than they were giving it.

(*MOLLY appears in the doorway.*)

MOLLY. My goodness, there's a whole crowd in here!

MEGAN. Hi Molly! I have your order right – here –

(*She goes to the counter and moves a large potted flowering plant to the front of the counter, starts to ring it up.*)

MOLLY. Oh my goodness that is just gorgeous. Isn't that something.

MEGAN. And I wanted to show you this. I think it's so beautiful.

(*She shows her an orchid.*)

MOLLY. Oh my goodness.

MEGAN. Doesn't it look like an angel?

MOLLY. It does!

MEGAN. It reminded me of you. I'm going to give it to you.

MOLLY. Oh.

LOU. You can't just give that away.

MEGAN. Of course I can.

LOU. That's not your plant.

MEGAN. Roger can I give this to Molly?

MOLLY. I can pay for it.

MEGAN. No no I work here for free, he'll let me do it.

LOU. That's an expensive plant.

MEGAN. It's worth like fifty bucks.

MOLLY. *(Sotto voce.)* A hundred and fifty.

ROGER. It's fine.

MOLLY. It's all right. I can pay for it.

MEGAN. *(Smitten with guilt now.)* No.

MOLLY. We should support small businesses! This is such
a nice shop, and everything on the street is just shutting
down and pretty soon we'll have nothing. I insist.

*(She hands **ROGER** her credit card.)*

*(To **ROGER**.)* You let me pay for it. I want to pay for it.

*(**ROGER** starts to ring it up.)*

LOU. How do you know Megan?

MEGAN. *(Admitting this.)* We are in a prayer group.

LOU. You're in a prayer group?

MEGAN. Yes. I'm in a prayer group. She invited me so
I went. I like it. It's very relaxing.

LOU. I ask you where you go, you never said "a prayer
group."

MEGAN. I just forgot to mention it.

LOU. I thought you weren't supposed to be lying all the
time. Don't they say that at A.A.? No lying?

MEGAN. I only went a couple times, Dad.

LOU. So that's a lie you only told a couple times.

MEGAN. It wasn't a lie. I just felt private about it.

LOU. So "private" is different than "lie."

MEGAN. I think it is.

LOU. Because they kind of look like the same thing from my viewpoint.

MEGAN. I'm not a child, Dad. I'm allowed to –

LOU. Oh you're "allowed"? By whom? By whom are you "allowed"?

(There is a terrible pause at that one.)

MOLLY. This is my fault.

LOU. I'm sorry, I don't even know who you are.

ROGER. This is one of my customers.

MEGAN. Molly. Her name is Molly.

MOLLY. Megan and I met here in the store a couple months ago –

LOU. Due respect, this is a complicated situation between me and my daughter, it's not something other people can participate in.

MEGAN. Dad.

LOU. Yes, what?

MEGAN. I apologize.

(A beat.)

I know how much you've done for me. I know how anxious it makes you.

LOU. It doesn't make me anxious.

MEGAN. That's not what I meant.

LOU. Then say what you mean!

MEGAN. I mean I know you've done a lot for me and I can never repay it and I'm really grateful and I apologize. For...

(She looks around, confused.)

ROGER. For the prayer meetings, you didn't tell him.

MEGAN. *(Quick.)* I apologize for not telling you about going to the prayer meetings. I know I should have. I understand why it seems disrespectful to you. That wasn't my intent. I won't do it again.

(A beat.)

LOU. There are rules to you living at my house. I didn't have to take you in.

MEGAN. I know, Dad.

LOU. I am not going down this road with you again. You are not putting me through all this, again.

*(There is a terrible pause at that. **MOLLY** tries to step in.)*

MOLLY. You can come as well, if you like. If you want to see who we are and what we're doing? People would love to have you. I would love to have you! Megan tells me that she's adopted and I would love to talk to you about that. I keep trying to talk to my husband about adoption and he just wants to work in the garden! It doesn't really makes sense to him but Megan tells me you were a terrific father and I'd love to hear about the adoption process.

LOU. She was her mother's biological kid. I just stepped in.

MOLLY. Not "just"! Megan told me so much about…

LOU. *(Bristling.)* Yeah?

MOLLY. Mostly we pray. It's a prayer group. It's very precious to all of us. As a way to support each other.

LOU. I'm not going to go pray with a bunch of women.

(Beat.)

ROGER. Megan, maybe you can help Molly carry these to her car.

MEGAN. Sure.

EVERETT. I could do that.

ROGER. You could if you worked here. Sadly, you don't.

> *(As **MEGAN** reaches for the purchase, **LOU** sees something on the counter.)*

LOU. What's this?

ROGER. Oh that's, nothing.

LOU. It's got her name on it.

MEGAN. My name?

ROGER. It's nothing, for the store.

LOU. If it's for the store, why does it have her name on it?

ROGER. It's just something I thought that she could take on as a project for the store.

LOU. You're putting her in charge of "projects" now?

ROGER. I told you, she's doing a good job.

LOU. So what's the project?

*(To **MEGAN**.)* What is it?

MEGAN. I don't know.

LOU. So open it.

ROGER. It's not really

LOU. Look. I'm her father. And due respect, they told me at the hospital I'm responsible and she has a history of substance abuse, I can't take that lightly. She's receiving packages away from the house? I don't know what's in there. I need to see what's in there.

> *(**LOU** is still hostile, not the least because now he's embarrassed. **ROGER** sighs, shrugs.)*

ROGER. Sure, she can open it. It's something I just thought she might like. It's kind of a present.

LOU. You said it was for the store.

ROGER. It is. It's for the store. It's also a present.

LOU. You bought her a present.

MEGAN. People are allowed to buy me presents, Dad!

EVERETT. He doesn't buy me presents.

ROGER. You don't work here anymore!

EVERETT. I'm just saying.

        (**MEGAN** *pulls out something white and huge.*)

ROGER. It's not really anything. It's just this thing I saw online.

LOU. What is it?

ROGER. It's nothing.

MEGAN. *(Overwhelmed.)* It's for bees.

EVERETT. Bees?

ROGER. I thought maybe we could keep bees.

LOU. This is going in the wrong direction.

MEGAN. *(Excited.)* Can I put it on?

ROGER. It's yours.

MOLLY. Well look at that.

MEGAN. Oh my god oh my god oh my god – can you help me? Can you –

MOLLY. Of course I can.

        (**MEGAN** *starts to put it on.* **MOLLY** *helps her.*)

LOU. You're keeping bees?

ROGER. I read up on it and I actually have a good setup for it in the garden out back. There's lots of room and you don't actually even need a permit. Or you can do it on the roof, all over the country people are exploring different approaches to urban apiculture. I haven't ordered the hives or the bees yet but most apiaries don't sell out until January or February so we have time to organize our plans around how we want to proceed. I don't know a lot about keeping bees per se but obviously there is a symbiosis between botany and apiology which we would be engaging more than figuratively. There is a serious ongoing concern about colony collapse nationally and so amateur beekeeping is actually encouraged by local governments, it's akin to composting or recycling on the list of environmental concerns that you can actually participate in. On a local level.

> (**MEGAN** *has the suit on.*)

MEGAN. Is this right? Is this right?

MOLLY. I think the gloves are supposed to clip on somewhere...

MEGAN. Isn't there supposed to be a hat? Where's the hat?

ROGER. Oh the hat came yesterday.

> (*He goes to get it in the back of the store.*)

LOU. You bought her a hat?

ROGER. (*Calling back.*) Well, you can't – you know if you're dealing with bees, you have to... Anyway.

> (*He hands it to* **MEGAN.** **MEGAN** *puts it on.*
> *Everyone watches.*)

MEGAN. How do I look?

> (*She turns to show it to them.*)

LOU. You look ridiculous.

>   *(The room is silent.)*

>   What? She looks ridiculous!

>   *(He leaves, annoyed.)*

MEGAN. I love it. I just love it.

>   *(She throws her arms around **ROGER**.)*

>   *(Blackout.)*

Scene Six

(Several days later.)

*(***ROGER*** at the counter, working. ***EVERETT*** is looking at some of the new plants. He is in fact loitering. ***ROGER*** watches him out of the corner of his eye.)*

ROGER. What do you want, Everett?

EVERETT. I'm looking for a plant, I need to buy a plant.

ROGER. You don't have enough plants? The marijuana business has taken a tumble recently?

EVERETT. As a matter of fact I've totally cleaned that up, Roger. I mean, I took your advice to heart, and I realize that my affection for ganja had gotten in the way of something that mattered to me even more.

ROGER. The truck?

EVERETT. You! It came between me and you. And now that you're doing so well, everyone can see that business is on the upswing here, I was thinking maybe you'd like to revisit our previous arrangement.

ROGER. Meaning?

EVERETT. You going to make me beg?

ROGER. No I'm not going to make you beg. I like it that you don't work here anymore. It's much nicer without you.

EVERETT. That's hilarious.

ROGER. I'm not trying to be funny.

EVERETT. All I'm saying, she's all about those bees now, the business is on more solid ground, you're going to need some help.

ROGER. Lou says I don't.

EVERETT. Lou is an accountant! And he doesn't much like her, did you not notice that because everyone else did.

ROGER. Your point being what?

EVERETT. I think you know my point.

ROGER. So you are once again wrong.

(A figure stands in the door. This is **ADAM**. *He is clean cut, very sure of himself.)*

EVERETT. I agree.

ROGER. You agree that you're wrong?

EVERETT. My point is, Lou is obsessed with all the wrong things! He's so negative, he just sees death everywhere! You and I, we see life!

ROGER. Shut up.

EVERETT. Just think about it.

ROGER. I'm not going to think about it.

EVERETT. Think about it.

(He goes, passing **ADAM** *in the door.* **ROGER** *takes the new guy in.)*

ROGER. Can I help you?

ADAM. I'm looking for Megan. She work here?

ROGER. She's in the back.

ADAM. Can you tell her I'm here?

ROGER. Who are you?

ADAM. She knows who I am.

(He goes and looks at a stand of plants. **ROGER** *is thinking about this when* **MEGAN** *enters. She is still wearing the bee suit.)*

MEGAN. I still cannot figure out how to get the gloves to fasten, Roger. Setting up the hive was easier by about a mile.

(*She stops when she sees* **ADAM.** *He looks at her.*)

What are you, what are you?

ADAM. What are you wearing?

MEGAN. I don't want to talk to you.

ADAM. I'm aware.

MEGAN. Roger can you tell him to go?

ROGER. You have to go.

ADAM. You don't have any standing in this conversation, whoever you are.

MEGAN. (*Furious.*) This is Roger! This is his shop!

ADAM. Megan. Megan. We have a lot of stuff we have to get through.

MEGAN. I am not talking to you!

ADAM. You are talking to me and if you won't do it here, you have to take that costume off and come with me to someplace we can talk.

MEGAN. (*To* **ROGER.**) Call the police.

ADAM. Do not do anything that stupid.

ROGER. She doesn't want you here. You have to get out of here.

ADAM. Then she's going to have to come with me. Or we're calling the police.

ROGER. I'm happy to call the police.

ADAM. You want to bring the police into this? Megan? Is that what you want? You want to drag all that all up again? 'Cause we can do that.

MEGAN. Why are you here if you don't want to drag it all up? Why are you here?

> *(She is really flipped. He is equivalently calm.)*

ADAM. If you want to do this here, I can do this here.

> *(He looks at* **ROGER**.*)*

Could we have some privacy?

ROGER. She says you should leave.

ADAM. That's not what she wants.

ROGER. Well, it's what I want and this is my store. Please go.

ADAM. Megan? I got to talk to you, and I'm not kidding. Tell him.

MEGAN. It's fine. It's fine.

ROGER. Is it?

> *(To* **MEGAN**.*)* Is that what you want? Megan. You have to tell me what to do.

MEGAN. *(Abrupt.)* I don't care. Yes. Do what he says. It's fine.

ROGER. Are you sure?

ADAM. She just said it.

MEGAN. It's fine Roger it's fine.

> *(***ROGER*** thinks about this.)*

ROGER. I'll be in the back.

> *(He goes. A moment.)*

ADAM. What are you wearing?

> *(***MEGAN*** strips off the beekeeping suit, suddenly.)*

MEGAN. Nothing.

ADAM. Yeah they told me they let you out of the hospital a couple months ago, it surprised the hell out of me.

MEGAN. What do you want, Adam? What do you, why are you here?

ADAM. Who's that guy, Roger? Your dad's friend? This is his place?

MEGAN. What do you want?

ADAM. I'd rather go someplace else.

MEGAN. I'm not going any place with you. Just say what you have to say and then get out of here.

ADAM. Oh that's nice.

MEGAN. I am being nice you piece of shit.

ADAM. They said you were better. I don't see it.

MEGAN. What do you want.

(She waits. He thinks about how to answer that.)

ADAM. We never talked about it. I need to talk about it.

MEGAN. What?

ADAM. I need to talk about what happened. To Henry.

MEGAN. Oh god. Please please don't do this. Please go away now.

ADAM. They told me I had to.

MEGAN. Who told you, what sick person told you to come here

ADAM. I'm not the one who's sick. And, I'm not leaving until we get through this.

MEGAN. I came here to get better. These are really nice people, Adam, and I'm getting better and you are not allowed to just come in here and make me make me you cannot do this to me anymore

ADAM. If you're better then why can't you talk about it. They told me that if you can't talk about it then you're lying to yourself.

MEGAN. I do talk about it, but I'm not talking to you about it.

ADAM. Why not. Why not. I'm the one you owe it to, more than anyone. And you just walked away.

MEGAN. I hardly just walked away

ADAM. After what you did to Henry, how he died, your own kid, did you even see

MEGAN. Of course I saw, I was the one who found him, you fuck

ADAM. Oh that's great

MEGAN. I was the one who found him and you

ADAM. And I what? I what? You stand there and tell me you got better. You're not allowed to get better after what you did.

MEGAN. STOP. YOU STOP.

> (**ROGER** *steps in.*)

ADAM. You get out of here. This has nothing to do with you.

MEGAN. I'm okay Roger I'm okay.

ROGER. Maybe we should call the police.

MEGAN. That won't be necessary. I can talk to him. I can do this.

> (**ROGER** *doesn't want to, but after a moment,*
> *he goes.*)

ADAM. That your boyfriend?

MEGAN. I'm not talking about Roger, he's none of your business.

ADAM. He's kind of old, isn't he?

MEGAN. Oh you leave him out of this.

ADAM. That's your type now? I mean no seriously. I wouldn't have guessed.

MEGAN. Is that why you came here? Because you couldn't stand to think that I might I might I might – LIVE – why are you here why don't you just tell me why you are here so I can get through this

ADAM. Look. I'm not here for retribution. Not that there could be retribution. But I am not here expecting you to make anything up to me. I just wanted to like acknowledge between us that this is what happened to our son. Because of what you did.

MEGAN. You want me to...

ADAM. Just acknowledge it. Acknowledge it to my face. You killed our son. Just say it.

  (A beat.)

MEGAN. *(Quiet.)* Why do you want that?

ADAM. Because they said I had to have it! To move on! What is the matter with you? You're like your brain is gone, Megan, you can't understand a simple sentence and you didn't use to be stupid like this, you were a total pain in my ass in plenty of other ways but stupid was never the issue. If anything you're too fucking smart. So stop acting like such a moron and just say it.

MEGAN. *(Dangerous.)* You think I won't say it to you? You hunted me down and came all this way just to make me say what happened and you think I won't do it?

ADAM. Oh, man. This sucks.

MEGAN. What did I ever see in you?

ADAM. Okay, I'm not actually looking for a full jaunt down memory lane.

MEGAN. You came here.

ADAM. I came here.

MEGAN. Because I lied before, you want to make sure I keep lying, is that what this is?

ADAM. Okay okay.

MEGAN. Who told you to find me.

ADAM. Look

MEGAN. Who is they? Who is they?

ADAM. Just say it.

MEGAN. Just tell me who they is. Who is they, these people who told you you had to come here and torture me, who are they?

ADAM. I'm getting married.

(*A beat.*)

MEGAN. Oh.

ADAM. And my wife

MEGAN. Your wife

ADAM. My girlfriend, my fiancée, she's great.

MEGAN. And she wanted you to come see me?

ADAM. Our therapist

MEGAN. You're in therapy before you're even married?

ADAM. Because of what happened. Because of what you did, yeah, that's right, everybody wants to make sure that I'm clear in my heart to get married and no one wants to think I'm just trying to replace my son

MEGAN. What do you mean, replace?

ADAM. Okay. Well, okay. She's pregnant. And people really want to know that I'm ready. So they asked me to come see you.

MEGAN. Why didn't you just lie?

ADAM. Okay.

MEGAN. You're such a colossal fucking liar about absolutely everything why couldn't you just lie about this, just tell them

ADAM. Okay

MEGAN. Just TELL THEM that you came here and saw me and I said whatever you wanted me to say, why didn't you just lie, why didn't you

ADAM. Because I'm trying to make a new life! Is that so insane, after what happened, I want to make a new life, I want to be an honest person?

MEGAN. Then be an honest person. You tell me what happened.

ADAM. Yeah, okay. I knew you were going to say that.

MEGAN. No, don't tell me. Don't tell me what happened. I can't... I can't...

ADAM. Here's the thing though, Megan, if you run around and try to talk to anybody about what happened

MEGAN. Is she the one you were with? When you left him in the car?

(*There is a terrible silence at that.* **ADAM** *shifts, uncomfortable.*)

ADAM. You said yourself to the police, you told the police

MEGAN. And now you're going to try and have another kid?

ADAM. You told the police that it was your fault and if you're going to change that story

MEGAN. Of course it was my fault I left him with you and you're a heartless evil fuck and what was I thinking, I never thought you'd leave him out in the car to die.

ADAM. You told them that you did it.

MEGAN. Because it was worse that you did it! Oh god. Oh god. I couldn't I didn't I never thought

ADAM. And I don't want you showing up and trying to come up with some new story to take revenge on me

MEGAN. Why did I do it? Why did I let you have him? I knew what you were. I knew the kind of person you were. I knew that I had to get away from you, I had to get Henry away from you.

ADAM. Don't start on that. I was a good father. I never hit him. I never hit you!

MEGAN. I was leaving you! I had left, I was taking him from you and I felt guilty so I let you have him just for one afternoon, I never thought you would, it's my fault it's my fault how could I have left him with you? Do you know what happened to him? I found him, I found him, he had torn his hair out, Adam!

ADAM. Okay.

MEGAN. He was purple! His face was covered in scratches –

ADAM. Stop it!

MEGAN. He was suffocated my little boy you suffocated him the inside of that car was a hundred and ten degrees and you left him in there for hours for HOURS

ADAM. I FORGOT.

MEGAN. You forgot.

ADAM. You shouldn't have left him with me. I wasn't used to like being the guy in charge. You knew that. And that's why, that's why – you know, that's why and I don't know why shit happens like that. I mean it was an accident. He was my kid too. And I feel bad. But seriously you shouldn't have left him with me. And, if anyone comes by and wants to talk to you about it, I hope you will stick with that story. That it's your fault, really, because you should not have left him with me and I understand why you feel the need to take the responsibility.

(*A beat.*)

MEGAN. Yes. I will continue to tell that story.

ADAM. Because it's the truth.

MEGAN. Do you need me to sign anything?

ADAM. I don't think so. They just wanted us to talk, clear the air.

(*Then.*)

You know, he's not suffering anymore, I think that's something to think about. And you were going to leave me anyway, huh? I don't think I fully knew that. I thought, you know, that you and I more or less fell apart because of what happened. So it's good to know that it was pretty much over before, you know.

(*Then.*)

I'm sorry you're still taking it so hard. I heard you were doing better.

(*He shrugs, looks around, goes.* **MEGAN** *is alone for a moment. She looks around, confused, picks up the beekeeper's outfit, holds it.* **ROGER** *enters, tentative.*)

MEGAN. Did you hear that? Were you listening?

ROGER. Well, I wasn't listening but I heard it.

(*Then.*)

Why do you let people think

MEGAN. Because it's worse! What I did was worse! I can't believe I left him with that man. And he did that. He left him in that hot car. And I came back and found him. And he was, he was

ROGER. You have to tell them.

MEGAN. Tell who? What would it matter? What would it change?

ROGER. It would change everything.

MEGAN. It would change nothing! Henry is still, he's still in that car, suffocating, he's dying because I left him with that monster, I gave him to him, I just –

ROGER. Stop it! Please stop. Stop.

(He goes to her, takes her by the shoulders and holds her. She calms down.)

MEGAN. I'm sorry.

(She starts to get a grip. He lets her go.)

ROGER. It's not your fault.

MEGAN. I'm his mom. I'm his Mom

ROGER. You didn't know.

MEGAN. I did know.

ROGER. You could not have known.

MEGAN. I knew what he was. And I left Henry with him, I left him

ROGER. You didn't do what they say you did.

MEGAN. No. No. I have to, it's fine the way it is. It's finished!

ROGER. It is clearly not finished and it shouldn't be. You have to call the police.

MEGAN. Why? Who says? It would make everything come back and he and he would he would

ROGER. It doesn't matter what he'd do, you have to tell them!

MEGAN. You saw him! He's a scary guy, everything slides off of him and that's him on a nice day! He was being relatively civil!

ROGER. Are you afraid of him?

MEGAN. Yes I'm afraid I can't god can't you just

ROGER. You have to

MEGAN. *(Snapping.)* I don't HAVE to do anything! It's all done, can't you understand that? It's done, it's OVER.

ROGER. It's not over.

MEGAN. *(Trying to stay on top of this.)* Look this is not this is not

ROGER. Not what?

MEGAN. Not helping!

ROGER. I don't choose to help.

MEGAN. Well, I choose – I choose –

ROGER. Your choice

MEGAN. Yes my choice

ROGER. Is to not be innocent.

MEGAN. I'm not innocent!

ROGER. You are innocent of this

MEGAN. He died! My little boy – died – in the most hideous – he was just a little boy. He was a little kid. He was my little kid.

> *(She looks at the beekeeper's outfit, tossed on the floor. She picks it up and gives it back to him.)*

You should send this back, see if you can get your money back.

ROGER. I don't want my money back.

MEGAN. It's a stupid idea, keeping bees. The bees are dying. Let them die.

ROGER. I will not let the bees die!

MEGAN. Do what you want with the fucking bees. I don't care.

ROGER. You are acting like a coward.

MEGAN. So what.

ROGER. You are acting like a liar.

MEGAN. I'm not a liar.

ROGER. You were the one, you told me

MEGAN. It doesn't matter what I told you.

ROGER. That if you don't tell the truth it will come up through the trap door and and and

MEGAN. You don't know anything about it!

ROGER. I know this is a lie, the worst lie anyone has ever told. This story you are letting everyone believe is a betrayal of your son. You dishonor him by letting people believe that you…you dishonor him.

(A pause.)

MEGAN. You don't know anything about anything. You're a crazy plant person. You hide in this stupid shop that no one comes to and you tell yourself it means something, it doesn't mean anything. People laugh at you because you're nothing.

ROGER. That is not

MEGAN. I'm not the coward. You're the coward. You hide from life. You let everyone push you around like some kind of moron or idiot, you you you're a freak. You're like a plant yourself. Why? Because you felt sorry for your mommy who couldn't even grow a carrot in her yard? You're still trying to make things okay for your mommy? Pathetic. It's worse than pathetic. What are you looking at?

ROGER. I'm looking at truth, which has come up through a trap door, and is eating a person alive.

MEGAN. Fuck you. You don't know anything. You fucking plant person

ROGER. Megan.

(She throws a plant at him, which stops him in his tracks.)

MEGAN. You don't know anything about anything.

(She goes. He stops, and picks up the plant.)

(Blackout.)

Scene Seven

(Night. The store is deserted.)

(The sounds of keys in the lock.)

EVERETT. I got it.

MEGAN. I got it I got it

*(The door opens. **MEGAN** pushes the door open, **EVERETT** right behind. They are laughing. They bump into the counter.)*

Look out!

EVERETT. It's dark.

MEGAN. Don't turn the light on.

*(She staggers, raises a bottle of scotch, drinks. Knocks something over in the dark. **EVERETT** laughs, lights up his vaporizer.)*

EVERETT. This is like high school.

MEGAN. Oh god I loved high school.

EVERETT. I bet you did.

*(That makes them both laugh. **EVERETT** takes a hit off his vaporizer. **MEGAN** grabs him.)*

MEGAN. Wait wait wait. I want some.

(She kisses him, sucks in the smoke. He laughs.)

EVERETT. You know I didn't think you liked me.

MEGAN. I don't, I think you're a complete idiot.

(That makes him laugh. They kiss again.)

I used to date complete idiots all the time. That was my food group. The stupider the better. You didn't think of it that way, you just thought he's kind of hot and then the next thing you know you're making out behind the science building. And it all felt great. People would get mad at you for shit that was so stupid like staying out all night or getting a C on a geometry test and it didn't feel like anything. It was...

>*(She looks around. The plant store in the darkness is breathing in a different way. Shadows loom and move. **EVERETT** is taking a hit off the vaporizer.)*

Where are we?

EVERETT. We're at the store. You said you wanted to come here. You were like totally determined.

MEGAN. Oh yeah.

EVERETT. You said you wanted to have sex with the plants.

MEGAN. Did I say that?

EVERETT. And I said, the plants? What about me?

MEGAN. What did I say then?

EVERETT. You told me it was entirely possible that I might get lucky.

MEGAN. That's what I used to say when I was trying to wriggle out of something.

EVERETT. You aren't wriggling out of anything.

>*(He kisses her. She staggers away again.)*

MEGAN. I wanted to have sex with Roger. He wouldn't do it. It was a solid no.

EVERETT. You wanted to have sex with Roger?

>*(He starts to laugh.)*

MEGAN. Why is that funny?

EVERETT. Get real. He's a virgin.

MEGAN. That's what I thought! But I don't think he is. I think he's...a saint.

EVERETT. Roger?

MEGAN. They pray to saints in that prayer group I went to. Everybody's got a saint. And the saints do things for them. Like if you're taking a trip, you pray to Saint Christopher! He has a little kid on his shoulder, like he's carrying a little kid somewhere. Like Saint Jude finds things. If you lose something, you pray to Saint Jude. It was terrible. Everything they said sounded like my life. All those nice ladies. They all felt sorry for me. They wanted to pray for me! So we prayed. Nothing changed.

(The lights shift. She looks around, frightened.)

EVERETT. So is that why you think Roger's a saint? Because nothing changes around here?

MEGAN. No no no. Everything changes. You start with nothing and then everything changes. You start with a little seed and then things grow.

EVERETT. They die you mean. You chop things up with the pruning shears until there's nothing left.

MEGAN. No, that's not...

EVERETT. Where have you been? This place is going under. Any normal person would sell it, he could make some real money, but he's like stuck in the past. This whole neighborhood is going to get grabbed up by some real estate developer, Roger's going to end up with nothing.

MEGAN. He doesn't have nothing. He has everything.

EVERETT. News to me.

(But the shadows are whispering now.)

MEGAN. Do you hear that?

EVERETT. Hear what?

MEGAN. It's the plants. The plants talk to him.

(She is serious, innocent, open.)

EVERETT. Oh yeah? What do they say?

MEGAN. I don't know. They don't talk to me. But they talk to Roger. I watch him, sometimes, he's listening to them, they're telling him things. I think it's about, things like air and water. And light.

EVERETT. Wow.

MEGAN. No no no. It's big. It's like a big version of that. And then there's something else. He touches them. And they tell him a secret.

EVERETT. Really.

MEGAN. I saw it.

EVERETT. You're nuts.

MEGAN. No no no. It's true. The plants know things that we can't ever know. And they tell them to Roger.

(She says it with just enough reverence to focus his attention.)

EVERETT. Are you in love with him? You're in love with *Roger*?

MEGAN. No. I don't love anybody.

EVERETT. Because that's a little creepy.

MEGAN. *(Surprised.)* Why?

EVERETT. It just is.

MEGAN. He's too holy for me.

EVERETT. Oh, "holy," that's what you call it.

MEGAN. You know what, no offense, but you're like a larva. You know, you're like something that's not even a bug yet. So I don't actually expect you to understand.

(*Then.*)

I tried to kill myself.

EVERETT. I heard.

MEGAN. You want to know what it felt like?

EVERETT. I thought you were just drinking and like doing pills.

MEGAN. No no no, this was different. It wasn't like I was pretending to just get wasted. I was doing it. Like if I had a gun, I would have done it that way. I wanted to know if God was out there. Because if God is there, then Henry is safe. And he still exists somewhere. And I just wanted to know that. So I thought if I could see God, if I could really piss him off, I'd see him, and then I'd know.

EVERETT. But then you'd never see your kid again. Because it's like a mortal sin, right? To kill yourself? Then you just go to hell.

MEGAN. I'm already in hell.

(**EVERETT** *thinks about that for a moment, but just a moment.*)

EVERETT. You know, not to be like unsympathetic, but I was having a little more fun a few minutes ago. And so were you.

(*He moves in on her.*)

MEGAN. Was I?

(*He straddles her. She lets him.*)

EVERETT. We both were. You said I was a complete idiot. And that you like complete idiots.

MEGAN. I can't remember.

EVERETT. Then let me remind you.

(He takes the bottle away from her, starts to kiss her. The plants rustle and whisper around her. He pushes her skirt up, undoes his jeans. She lets him.)

(He starts to move on top of her.)

*(The door opens. **ROGER** steps in, sees them.)*

ROGER. What are you doing.

EVERETT. Fuck. Roger.

ROGER. Get off of her. GET OFF OF HER.

*(**EVERETT** scrambles away from **MEGAN** as **ROGER** steps in, looks away.)*

EVERETT. Look, this this wasn't my idea. Megan said she wanted to come here.

(He is scrambling to get his pants back on.)

Megan! Tell him!

(She is silent.)

ROGER. Megan? Megan.

(He goes to her. She has passed out.)

What did you do. You little shit.

EVERETT. I didn't do anything! I told you, this was her idea!

ROGER. Megan. Megan.

MEGAN. I'm okay.

(But she is barely conscious.)

EVERETT. I bumped into her at the coffee joint, she said she was having a bad day, she just wanted someone to talk to.

ROGER. So you took her out and got her drunk.

EVERETT. Hey. She's an adult, she does what she wants. She wanted to come here and have sex with the plants. That's what she said. I mean, she's crazy. Everybody knows it. You let a crazy person into your life and shit is going to happen, Roger. That's all I'm saying. She killed her own kid. What do you expect.

> **(ROGER** *looks at him.)*

You're not going to call the cops are you? Because people get so bent out of shape around something like this but I'm telling you Roger seriously, this was consensual, it was all her idea. She was fine a second ago; she really was.

> *(A beat.)*

You're not going to call the cops are you?

ROGER. You take advantage. You take advantage of a person whose heart is broken, you deserve worse than anything I can do to you.

EVERETT. Great.

> *(He splits.)*

ROGER. *(Quiet.)* Megan? Come on. Come on.

> **(ROGER** *sits her up and tenderly helps her walk to the door. Blackout.)*

Scene Eight

*(The following morning. **ROGER** is in the shop, cleaning up the mess that Megan and Everett made the night before.)*

*(**MOLLY** enters.)*

MOLLY. Hello!

ROGER. We're not open.

MOLLY. You're not? The door was open.

ROGER. Guess I forgot to lock it last night.

(He goes to lock it.)

MOLLY. Goodness. Look at this place!

(She sees the mess, steps in.)

ROGER. We're not open!

MOLLY. I'm not really here to buy anything. I just wanted to check in on Megan. She didn't make the prayer meeting last night and she had said she was going to come.

ROGER. She's not here.

MOLLY. When she gets in will you let her know I stopped by?

ROGER. I don't know when I'll see her.

MOLLY. Well, when she gets in. Oh what happened to this poor baby?

*(She holds up one of the plants that got knocked over. **ROGER** takes it from her, annoyed.)*

ROGER. It's not a baby. It's a chimeras varietal saintpaulia.

(A beat.)

ROGER. Commonly known as an African violet.

MOLLY. I just meant it looks like it could use a little help.
Guess you'll have to work your magic on it.

(He throws it away.)

ROGER. I don't like African violets. They show off.

MOLLY. Are you all right?

ROGER. I'm fine. I'm just very busy and, I'm just very busy.

MOLLY. What's the matter, Roger?

ROGER. Just go.

*(She goes. **ROGER** goes back to the counter.
He tries to organize the things that are there
but he can't focus. He goes back and gets the
African violet out of the trash can, tries to fix
it, fails. He sets it down, anguished. After a
moment, he sits, bewildered.)*

(There is a knock on the door.)

(Exploding.) WE'RE CLOSED.

*(There is another knock at the door. He turns
to look. **MEGAN** is there. He turns his back
on her, ignores her. She knocks again. He
continues to ignore her. She knocks again.)*

We're closed WE'RE CLOSED.

*(He goes, unceremoniously unlocks the door
and steps away. She enters. He goes to the
counter, his back to her.)*

We're not open.

MEGAN. Okay.

(She locks the door.)

ROGER. And, you're fired.

MEGAN. You can't fire me. You don't pay me.

ROGER. I don't want you here. That's what I mean by "you're fired."

MEGAN. I don't blame you.

ROGER. It would be remarkable if you did.

(He goes back to the counter, his back to her. She shifts on her feet. He turns and sees her there.)

Is there something else that we need to talk about? Because I'm pretty sure I've been clear. I don't want you here. I don't want your mess. I don't want any of this. Is that clear?

MEGAN. You're clear, you're totally clear.

ROGER. So?

MEGAN. We had a fight yesterday.

ROGER. Oh that's what you call that.

MEGAN. What would you call it?

ROGER. I don't have to call it anything because you don't work for me anymore.

MEGAN. Well, I need to apologize. I was upset and I said some things I didn't mean and I apologize.

ROGER. I do not accept your apology.

MEGAN. Okay. I don't blame you as I said. There is no excuse for the things I said, Roger. I mean it.

ROGER. I'm not arguing with you.

(Then.)

ROGER. Is that it?

MEGAN. I guess so.

> *(She starts for the door. Then stops.)*

Can you...um. Can you tell me what happened last night?

(Ashamed.) Because I don't remember.

> *(There is a terrible pause at this.* **ROGER** *looks at her.)*

ROGER. You don't remember.

MEGAN. I fell off the wagon. I remember that. And then this morning, Dad said you brought me home. But I don't remember anything else. I mean I remember that idiot Everett showing up and having drinks with him and then after that nothing. I kind of...blacked out.

ROGER. You blacked out.

MEGAN. Yes.

ROGER. *(Quiet.)* Well, that is just...unacceptable.

MEGAN. *(Still ashamed, but defensive.)* It is what it is.

ROGER. Is this what you choose for your life? This drinking, this belligerence, this chaos – is this what you choose?

MEGAN. No. I don't – I don't – choose it.

ROGER. Because it looks like you choose it. And I do not choose it. I do not let people walk all over me.

MEGAN. I know you don't.

ROGER. I am not an idiot who lets people push me around.

MEGAN. I know.

ROGER. People do what they do. I understand that. No. I do not understand it. I accept it. I accept things. But not everything.

MEGAN. I see.

ROGER. If you saw, you would have left by now.

> *(He turns his back on her again and goes back to work.)*

MEGAN. Listen, what happened, yesterday afternoon, my ex-husband showing up like that and everything coming back at me, it really it it it threw me

ROGER. *(Dogged.)* I was here.

MEGAN. I know you were here.

ROGER. It isn't any excuse!

MEGAN. I didn't say it was an excuse.

ROGER. And yet you are still here!

MEGAN. Hey I fell off the wagon! It's not the end of the world. You have to start all over with those stupid chips and now I don't have eighty-seven I only have one. And I'm mad at myself about that I'm really pissed about only having one fucking chip. I don't even have one chip. I have to make it to the end of the day to get one chip. But that doesn't mean

ROGER. What. What doesn't it mean.

MEGAN. I don't know I just

ROGER. You just what?

MEGAN. Could you – I mean, please. Please.

ROGER. Please what.

MEGAN. You're just you're not being very nice.

ROGER. I don't choose to be nice.

MEGAN. Okay. Okay, whatever I did, it was bad, I can see that. I I I apologize.

ROGER. I have already told you, I don't accept your apology.

MEGAN. Jesus. What did I do? I mean it. What did I do?

ROGER. *(Pissed.)* You put yourself in danger. And you put me in danger. You put everything in danger! Everything and everyone. And when you put other people in danger, they die. Plants die. The world dies. That's what you do.

>   *(She gasps, takes a step back.* **ROGER** *realizes what he said.)*

That's not – I should not have said that. I didn't mean that. I didn't mean what it sounded like I meant.

MEGAN. It sounded like what it sounded like.

ROGER. I wasn't talking about

MEGAN. About what? What weren't you talking about?

>   *(Her belligerence is rising.)*

ROGER. Megan.

MEGAN. You don't know a fucking thing. You don't know anything about anything except PLANTS.

>   *(In a heartbeat, he tries to save her as the speed of the argument ricochets in the opposite direction.)*

ROGER. Megan. You are not responsible for

MEGAN. For what?

ROGER. You are not responsible

MEGAN. I am responsible! Go to a fucking A.A. Meeting! It's rule number one! You're responsible for all of it!

ROGER. You are not responsible for the fact that things die.

MEGAN. Not things. People.

ROGER. Okay people. Neighborhoods. Hope. Children.

MEGAN. Not any children. Not general children. My child. My little boy. Henry.

ROGER. Everything dies.

MEGAN. Great. I feel much better now that we cleared that up.

ROGER. I'm not here to make you feel better. Why do you expect me to make you feel better, why do you expect me to know things? I don't know anything! I know about plants! I don't know anything else!

MEGAN. Well good we agree about something finally because you know what, Roger? You're no saint.

ROGER. I never said I was.

MEGAN. Well you're not.

(She starts to leave. He steps in her way.)

ROGER. Wait.

MEGAN. Get out of my way, Roger, you've been trying to get me to leave for weeks and I'm GOING now so get out of my fucking way!

(He doesn't move.)

What. What?

ROGER. I apologize.

*(A beat. **MEGAN** wants to dismiss that but she cannot, finally.)*

I spoke hastily and unkindly. You didn't deserve it. You have been a good employee, and I hurt you. So I apologize.

(There is another moment while she considers that.)

ROGER. In my anger, I implied something terrible, that I
didn't mean.

> *(A beat.)*

You did not kill your son.

MEGAN. I did, Roger. I did.

ROGER. Megan, you didn't. And you have to choose to
understand that, or you will die. And that would be a
waste. You're good at this. You're good with the plants.
You're good with the customers. I I I everybody says
I should sell the place and honestly I was starting to
think about it, because I didn't think I could make
it work without you. But I think we can, there are
customers coming more and more and and the beehives
are necessary, people need them, we need the bees, the
earth needs the bees.

MEGAN. The earth?

ROGER. The earth will claim us both soon enough.
I cannot run the store without you. And, I apologize.

> *(She thinks about this. She turns, takes the
> place in. Looks down.)*

MEGAN. I accept your apology.

ROGER. Thank you.

> *(They both wait, unsure of what to do next.)*

MEGAN. *(Finally.)* What happened to the African violet?

ROGER. It needs help.

> *(He looks at it, picks it up, holds it out to her.)*

But it can be saved, I think. It just needs to be repotted.

> *(After a moment, she takes it.)*

> *(Fade to black.)*

www.ingramcontent.com/pod-product-compliance
Lightning Source LLC
Chambersburg PA
CBHW070633120726
47909CB00004B/1424